MW01181094

Randy Johnson

ARIZONA HEAT!

by
Larry Stone

SPORTS PUBLISHING INC.
www.SportsPublishingInc.com

Production manager: Susan M. McKinney
Cover design: Scot Muncaster
Photos: *The Associated Press* and the University of Southern California

ISBN: 1-58261-042-8
Library of Congress Catalog Card Number: 99-61951

SPORTS PUBLISHING INC.
SportsPublishingInc.com

Printed in the United States.

CONTENTS

Randy helped lead the Mariners to their first playoff appearance in 1995. (AP/Wide World Photos)

CHAPTER ONE

Standing Tall

Randy Johnson knew the game on October 2, 1995, was one that would forever shape his stature as one of baseball's premier pitchers. He barely slept the night before, awakening every time he heard his 10-month-old daughter, Samantha, make a sound over the baby monitor on a nightstand next to his bed.

When Randy showed up at Seattle's Kingdome, his teammates on the Mariners noticed immediately the bad look on his face—and they were delighted. They had learned long ago that the crankier

Randy was, the better he usually pitched. And they had never needed him more than they did on this day.

"It was the biggest game of my career, and I knew I had to rise to the occasion," Randy said later. "This is the kind of game you find out a lot about yourself."

It was easily the most important game in Mariners history. The Mariners and California Angels had finished in a tie for the American League's Western Division title, just the third tie in AL history. The Mariners, who trailed the Angels by 13 games on August 2, had mounted one of the greatest comebacks in history, but after building a three-game lead over the Angels in the final week, they had fallen back by losing their final two games in Texas.

The Angels, meanwhile, won their final five games to catch Seattle and force the one-game playoff at the Kingdome. The winner would advance to the playoffs against the Yankees. The loser would go home, its season finished.

The Mariners had never made the playoffs in their 19-year history, but it was crucial that they do so now. The team was losing millions of dollars each year at the Kingdome, and management claimed that without a new stadium the team would have to move to another city. The Mariners' sensational performance late in the season had ignited baseball fever in the community, but many feared that their drive for a new ballpark would fail if they were eliminated by the Angels.

More than 50,000 noisy fans crammed into the Kingdome to watch Randy go up against Angels ace Mark Langston. Ironically, the two pitchers had been involved in the biggest trade in Mariner history in 1989. Langston, at the time Seattle's most successful pitcher ever, had gone to the

The tallest player in major-league history at 6-10, Randy is nicknamed "The Big Unit." (AP/Wide World Photos)

Montreal Expos for three young pitching prospects. One of them was Johnson, whose only claim to fame at the time was being, at 6 feet, 10 inches, the tallest player in major-league history. Most Mariners fans had hated the trade, believing the team had practically given away the popular Langston.

For awhile, it looked like they might be right. Because of his height, Randy had trouble learning proper pitching mechanics, and his control was poor. For three consecutive years (1990-92), he led the league in walks. He could be terribly inconsistent, pitching a shutout one start and then getting bombed the next.

But Randy, nicknamed "The Big Unit" for his size, had gradually developed into the league's most fearsome pitcher. Not only could he throw the ball up to 100 miles an hour, but with his flowing hair, fierce scowl and long stride to the plate, he was an intimidating presence on the mound. He finally learned how to control his pitches. The death of his father, Bud—his best friend—on Christmas Day, 1992, had brought tremendous grief, but also provided a new focus to his career.

And 1995 was his best season yet. Randy's record going into the Angels' game was 17 wins and just two losses! He was determined to prove that he deserved to be considered one of the best pitchers in the league.

"When he stepped on the field today, there was something about him," Mariner outfielder Ken Griffey Jr. said afterwards. "It was like, 'Give me one run and I'll take care of the rest.'"

Randy was up to the task, despite pitching on just three days rest, one fewer than normal. He had a perfect game going for 5⅔ innings, meaning he had retired the first 17 batters he faced, striking out nine. Langston was tough, too, and neither team had scored heading into the fifth inning. The Mariners pushed across one run in that inning, and then finally broke the game open with eight more runs in the final two innings for a 9-1 victory.

Randy was sensational, winding up with a three-hitter and 12 strikeouts. Mariners manager Lou Piniella considered taking out him for the final two innings to save his arm for the playoffs, but Randy badly wanted a complete game, so Piniella left him out there. In the ninth inning, the Kingdome crowd was on its feet, roaring for each pitch. When Randy struck out Tim Salmon to end the game, hundreds of fans poured onto the field. Some kissed home plate, while others stuffed their pockets with dirt from the infield.

Randy screamed, "Yes!" and threw his arms in the air. As he did after all his big victories, he pointed toward the sky, a silent tribute to his father. On this, the biggest day of his career, the only regret was that his dad wasn't in the ballpark to see it.

Randy, the youngest of six children, is very close to his mother, Carol. (AP/Wide World Photos)

Growing Up

When Randy Johnson signed his first long-term contract after the 1993 season, a four-year, $20.25 million deal, he spoke lovingly of his parents. Before his death, Bud had been a policeman in Livermore, California, southeast of Oakland. Carol was a homemaker. Randy, born on September 10, 1963, was the youngest of six children.

"Mom was the one who got me to my first Little League tryout on time," Randy said. "My happiest days in baseball might have been when my dad would come right to games after work, still dressed in his policeman's uniform."

Randy said of his dad, who stood 6-6: "He had two bad knees, but he'd get down on the asphalt to catch me. After I'd throw 15 over his head, he'd tell me, 'It's your turn to go get the ball.'

"He was my best friend and my biggest critic, a stern man who always wanted your best."

When he came home from work, Bud would ask young Randy if he had finished his chores, such as taking out the garbage or mowing the lawn.

"I'd say, 'No,' and he'd say, 'That's your job,'" Randy told the *Seattle Post-Intelligencer* years later. "I used to look at it as harping. But that wasn't the case at all. He was giving me some discipline and responsibility. He was trying to embed that into me for a later time, when things were going to be much more important in my life."

As a child growing up in the East Bay of Northern California, Randy naturally rooted for the great Oakland A's teams, which won three straight World Series championships from 1972-74. When he was 8, Randy would pretend he was Vida Blue, the left-handed star pitcher for the A's, as he threw a tennis ball against the garage at his family's home in Livermore. He threw so hard that the nails started to come loose. His dad reminded Randy to have a mallet handy so he could pound the nails back in.

By his own admission, Randy had a rough childhood. Always much taller than his classmates, he was self-conscious of his height, particularly after he shot up from 6-2 to 6-9 between seventh and 12th grade. He has said that he felt at times like "part of a freak show" as a teenager because of the way everyone stared at him. "I was the object of everyone's jokes and teases, and it hurt," he once told a reporter. "But it wasn't within my personal-

Randy is interviewed by 10-year-old Sean Treeder for Seattle's Kid Star Radio. (AP/Wide World Photos)

ity to lash out, so instead I went into a shell, became very defensive. I felt like I was growing up in the center of a three-ring circus."

Before his baseball skills blossomed, Randy wanted to be a police officer like his father. Though he always loved baseball, his Little League career got off to a tough start. Randy was late for the first game and couldn't find his team. Eventually, he went home in tears.

"In Little League, the kids were afraid when he pitched," Bill Geyer, a longtime Little League coach in Livermore, recalled in 1995. "But back at age 11 and 12, it wasn't that he threw hard, because he didn't yet. But he was 5 feet 9 when the rest of them were 5-1, maybe 5-2. He was so much bigger."

It wasn't until high school that Randy's fastball began to whiz by hitters. He rarely knew where it was going, but his velocity—more than 90 mph—made him a star pitcher by the time he was a senior

After high school, Randy declined an offer from the Atlanta Braves, accepting a scholarship from the University of Southern California instead. (University of Southern California)

at Livermore High School. Dozens of major league scouts attended Livermore's games. In his final start, Randy threw a perfect game, striking out 13. Overall, he struck out 121 batters in just 66⅓ innings. He was also a star basketball player at Livermore High, leading the league in scoring his senior year and making the all-league team. In one game, he scored 51 points.

After Randy's senior year, the Atlanta Braves selected him in the fourth round of the 1982 amateur draft. They offered him a $48,000 bonus, but Randy and his parents decided he should accept a scholarship to the University of Southern California, where the legendary coach Rod Dedeaux coveted his pitching skills.

He also went out for the USC basketball team, but after playing minimally his freshman and sophomore years, he gave up basketball to concentrate on baseball. One of his baseball teammates at USC

At USC, one of Randy's teammates was Mark McGwire. (University of Southern California)

was Mark McGwire, who would go on to set the major-league home-run record with 70 in 1998. In 1997, Mark hit a mammoth 538-foot home run off Randy at the Kingdome.

At USC, Randy exhibited the same intensity that would mark his major-league career. He often talked to himself on the mound and gestured wildly after big plays. He developed a reputation as a "flake" —someone prone to wacky behavior. As a freshman, in his collegiate debut against Stanford, he entered the game in relief. When he got to the mound he told Dedeaux he planned to pitch from a stretch to hold the baserunner close to first base. Dedeaux gently informed him that there was no runner at first base; the person he was looking at was Stanford's first-base coach.

"My God, he threw hard," Dedeaux recalled recently. "And he was delightful, naive and seemed to think life was a lot of fun."

Even though he still had problems with his control,
Randy showed off a big-league fastball at USC.
(University of Southern California)

It was at USC that Johnson also perfected his lifelong passion for photography. He took pictures for the *Daily Trojan,* the student newspaper. He has become an accomplished photographer whose work has been exhibited at shows and galleries.

In 1996, Randy was hired by the Pinnacle baseball card company to shoot a set of cards featuring star major-league players in unusual poses. For instance, he shot Will Clark in full uniform—as well as cowboy boots and a hat. On road trips, he often wakes up early to walk around the city with his camera, looking for intriguing shots. He once found a car that had been discarded in a dumpster and took a picture of it. With the Mariners, he published a calendar of his photos with the proceeds benefitting the homeless.

Wildness continued to plague Randy at USC. He established a school record by walking 104 batters in 1985, his junior year, to go along with a disappointing 6-9 record and a 5.32 earned-run-average. But he displayed a major-league fastball and was ranked the fourth-best college pitching prospect in a poll of scouts conducted by *Baseball America*.

"I was a true wild man in college," Randy said once. "I'd walk two guys, then strike out the side. I was raw. I never learned a lot of mechanics. "

He showed enough promise, however, that the Montreal Expos selected him in the second round of the 1985 draft after Randy's junior year at USC. While disappointed he didn't get picked in the first round, Randy signed with Montreal. His road to the big leagues had begun.

3

Breaking in

For the Expos, Randy was an intriguing specimen. His fastball was one of the liveliest anybody had ever seen, but his mechanics were a mess, and his personality was volatile. The Expos knew he had tremendous potential, but no one was quite sure if he would ever achieve it.

Randy's first assignment that summer was Montreal's single-A team in Jamestown, New York, where he came down with a sore arm and struggled to an 0-3 record. In 1986, he improved to 8-7 with a 3.16 ERA for West Palm Beach in the Florida

State League, striking out 133 in 120 innings but walking a league-leading 94. Pitcher Brian Holman, who came up with Randy and later pitched with him in Seattle, remembered one game that year in which an opposing hitter started to walk out to the mound to challenge Randy after a pitch that sailed over his head. Holman says that Randy pointed a finger at him and said, "Don't come out here, or I'll take your life." The batter returned to the plate.

In 1987, the Expos assigned pitching instructor Joe Kerrigan to work closely with Randy on his mechanics. Pitching for double-A Jacksonville, Florida, he averaged 10 strikeouts per nine innings, but he also averaged eight walks. Some baseball people feared that Randy's control problems were going to wipe out his career.

Early in his career, Randy drew interest more for his height than his pitching, which always upset him. At Triple-A Indianapolis, the public address announcer often introduced him as "the world's tallest pitcher." As was the case in high school and college, Randy often felt like he was a freak on display. With his animated behavior on and off the field, he brought some of it on himself.

Midway through the 1988 season, the Expos were on the verge of calling Randy up to the majors. But pitching in a minor-league game for Indianapolis, he was hit on his left wrist by a line drive. He was so angry at the prospect that his career had been jeopardized that he smashed his right hand on the bat rack in the dugout. While his wrist injury turned out to be moderate, he fractured his right hand and was sidelined for six weeks.

A few days later, a notice appeared on a bulletin board in Indianapolis' clubhouse and throughout the Expos' minor-league system: "Anybody in this organization who does something hasty to inhibit his ability will be fined." Below the note was written: "THE RANDY JOHNSON RULE."

Randy hugs Mariners catcher John Marzano after another win for the Big Unit. (AP/Wide World Photos)

Once his hand recovered, Randy finally got his major-league call in September of 1988 and made the most of it. In his first start on September 15, he beat the Pirates, and followed with a complete-game, 11-strikeout victory over the Cubs. When he walked to the mound for the first time, Randy officially became the tallest player in major-league history. It used to be 6-9 Johnny Gee, who pitched for the Pirates and Giants in the 1940s.

One day in spring training, Montreal outfielder Tim Raines had nearly collided with Randy while doing wind sprints. "Man, you're a big unit, aren't you?" Raines said. A nickname was born.

Randy went 3-0 in four starts for Montreal, striking out 25 batters in 26 innings. Most impressive, he walked only seven. The Expos were so impressed that they made plans to insert him into their starting rotation for the following year. At age 25, Randy had made it—or so it seemed.

Randy faces numerous requests for autographs at Seattle's spring training facility in Arizona. (AP/Wide World Photos)

Moving West

In spring training of 1989, Randy expressed optimism that he was up to the task of being one of Montreal's five starting pitchers, despite just 20 days of major-league experience. "It took me awhile to get control of my body, to find a delivery that would keep my arms and legs in sync with the rest of me," he said. "But I'm ready now. I'm ready upstairs, too."

But it wasn't a smooth rookie season at all. The Expos had a strong team that year, one they felt was capable of winning the National League's Eastern Division title. When Randy struggled early in the season, jumping out to an 0-4 record with a 6.69 ERA after six starts, they weren't in a position to display patience. Instead, in early May, he was sent back to the minor leagues to work out his mistakes. Randy had fallen victim to his old wildness problem, walking 26 batters in 29⅔ innings.

Meanwhile, the Expos were among the teams trying to acquire Mark Langston, ace left-hander of the Seattle Mariners. Langston was going to be a free agent the next year and the Mariners felt they couldn't afford to re-sign him. They decided it was better to trade him than to let him walk away after the season.

Several teams tried to obtain Langston, including the Boston Red Sox, Toronto Blue Jays, Los Angeles Dodgers, New York Mets and San Francisco Giants. But on May 25, Langston was traded to Montreal for three pitching prospects—Brian

Holman, Gene Harris, and a 6-10 left-handed fireballer named Randy Johnson. Just a year earlier, the Expos had told teams that Randy was an "untouchable"—they wouldn't trade him under any circumstances.

The Mariners decided to put Randy on their major-league roster. When he arrived in Seattle, manager Jim Lefebvre told him, "You're going to pitch every five days," and tried to reassure him that he didn't expect him to "replace" Langston.

In his American League debut, Randy pitched six strong innings to earn a victory over the New York Yankees at Yankee Stadium. Rookie outfielder Ken Griffey Jr. helped his cause with two home runs in Seattle's 3-2 victory. No one knew it yet, but Randy and Ken would become the most productive players in Mariner history.

Lefebvre saw enough of a spark in Randy after that first game to tell reporters, "He has the potential to be the dominant pitcher in all of baseball."

The trade was not popular in Seattle, but Randy helped change that perception by going 3-0 with a 1.31 ERA in his first three starts. Holman also pitched well. Randy finished the season with a 7-9 record for Seattle, leaving more questions than answers about his future. The first exclamation point of his career was still to come.

C H A P T E R   F I V E

Peaks and Valleys

Standing on the mound at the Kingdome facing the Detroit Tigers, Randy couldn't believe how much in sync he felt with Mariners catcher Scott Bradley. Every time Bradley put down a sign, Randy was already gripping the pitch that Bradley had called. It was June 2, 1990, and Randy was about to make history.

Inning after inning, the Tigers failed to get a hit. When he struck out Mike Heath for the final out of a 2-0 Seattle victory, Randy had pitched the first no-hitter in Mariners' history! It was just the

On June 2, 1990, Randy pitched the first no-hitter in Mariners history. (AP/Wide World Photos)

third complete game, and first shutout, of his career. Randy struck out eight (while walking six), and Seattle's radar gun showed that the fastest pitch he threw all night was the last one, a 97 mph fastball.

"I'm exhausted, but ecstatic I was able to do something like this," Randy said.

The pitching gem signalled to the baseball world that Randy was close to completing the transition from a wild thrower to a pitcher. He was already establishing himself as one of the game's most flamboyant personalities. When Randy arrived in Seattle from Montreal, he stripped yellow police tape around his locker. One day, he showed up in the dugout wearing a conehead. He became one of the leading practical jokers on the Mariners, once dousing teammate Jay Buhner with a carton of milk.

An enthusiast of heavy-metal music, Randy befriended many rock musicians, and even purchased his own set of drums to bang on. His animated

In Seattle, Randy became known as one of baseball's flamboyant personalities. (AP/Wide World Photos)

style on the mound began to attract Mariner fans, though opposing players weren't always pleased when he would gesture excitedly after a big strikeout. He could be outspoken, too. In 1990, he criticized Lefebvre, saying that he and Mariner pitching coach Mike Paul "don't know how to use a pitching staff yet." In 1994, he questioned Griffey's work habits.

Though still struggling with his control, Randy made his first All-Star team in 1990 (he didn't pitch in the game at Wrigley Field) and finished with a 14-11 record. What Randy and the Mariners wanted now was a breakthrough to the next level, so that he could become the consistently winning pitcher they knew he was capable of being.

That was to take another struggle. Randy went 13-10 in 1991, averaging nearly two walks more per nine innings than anyone else in the American League. Hinting of a problem to come, he was sidelined briefly with a sore back. One of Randy's highlights was a one-hit shutout win over Oakland. He took a no-hitter into the ninth inning before Mike Gallego led off with a single. In 1992, he struggled again to a 12-14 record despite winning his first of four consecutive strikeout titles with 241.

"I feel I'm reverting to the Randy Johnson of old, and I've worked too hard to bury him to let that happen," Randy said after a frustrating 12-4 loss to Toronto.

After another loss to Baltimore, new Mariner manager Bill Plummer claimed that Randy "quit on us" by asking to come out of the game at the end of the second inning.

It was near the end of the 1992 season that one of the most significant events of Randy's career took place. Before a game on August 7 against the Texas Rangers in Seattle, Randy had a long talk with the legendary Nolan Ryan, the greatest power pitcher of the era, and the Texas pitching coach, Tom House. They gave him a key mechanical tip about landing on the ball of his right foot instead of his heel during his windup. More important, Nolan talked with Randy about pitching strategies and philosophies—setting up hitters, keeping his composure and never giving in. Like Randy, Ryan had struggled with his control early in his career, and his words hit home.

"I gained momentum and confidence on the mound," Randy said.

Randy was a different pitcher the rest of the year—and the rest of his career, it turned out. He cut his walks nearly in half. He won four straight games in August and struck out 10 or more seven times to wrap up the first strikeout title. On September 28—pitching against Ryan, appropriately —Randy struck out 18 batters in just eight innings, tying the American League record for left-handers.

From 1992-1995, Randy won four straight strikeout titles. (AP/Wide World Photos)

Because he had already thrown 160 pitches, Randy decided not to work the ninth inning.

Ryan and Randy reunited over the winter to make an instructional video, "The Art of the Fastball." It gave Randy another invaluable opportunity to talk about pitching with the old master. Late in the 1993 season, Ryan's last, Randy honored Nolan by pitching a game against Texas wearing No. 34, Ryan's number.

That winter another event occurred that would have far-reaching ramifications on Randy's pitching and personal life.

Randy was so devastated by his father's death in 1992 that he considered quitting baseball. (AP/Wide World Photos)

CHAPTER SIX

Breaking Through

On Christmas Day, 1992, Randy flew to California to join his family. He brought his steady girlfriend, Lisa. Both his professional and personal life had never been better, and he was happy with the direction of his life. When they arrived, Randy received terrible news. His father, Bud, had suffered an aortic aneurysm—a heart attack. Randy rushed to the hospital, hoping to at least have a final moment with his dad. He was too late. When Randy arrived at the hospital, he was told the devastating news—his father had died.

Weeping, Randy put his head on his father's chest and said, "Why'd you have to go now? It's not time."

So distraught was Randy that he contemplated quitting baseball, but his mom, Carol, talked him out of it. The 1993 season turned out to be the breakthrough year of Randy's career. He went 19-8, led the major leagues with 308 strikeouts (just the 12th pitcher in history to surpass 300) and finished second to Jack McDowell of the Chicago White Sox in the voting for the Cy Young Award, given to the league's top pitcher.

Significantly, he reduced his walks to 99, the first full season he had been under 100. The pitching lessons he had received from Ryan helped tremendously. But Randy said it was his father's death that changed his outlook.

"My heart got a lot bigger," he said. "I have been able to get out of situations because I've allowed myself to dig a little deeper."

Another significant event in Randy's life that year was his marriage to Lisa, a former manager of a photo shop whom he met at a charity golf tournament in 1988. The couple now has three children—Samantha, born in 1994; Tanner, born in 1996; and Willow, born in 1998.

"You can't be selfish anymore," he said. ''It makes me realize how my mom and dad made sacrifices for us, too. Hopefully, I can be half the dad he was and try to raise my family the way my parents raised me.''

It was also after the 1992 season that trade rumors involving Randy first heated up, an occurrence that would continue nearly non-stop until he finally was traded to the Houston Astros in July of 1998. The Mariners were a financially struggling team, and Randy's contract had grown to $2.5 million, making him a prime candidate for relocation despite his increasing success. In the midst of his

In 1993, Randy was selected for the American League All-Star team. (AP/Wide World Photos)

great 1993 season, he was nearly traded at the July 31 trade deadline, and again after the season. But in December, the Mariners signed Randy to a four-year contract with a fifth-year option that was worth $26 million.

One of the most remembered moments of Randy's career occurred at the 1993 All-Star Game. Facing John Kruk of the Philadelphia Phillies, Randy's first pitch slipped out of his hand and flew directly over Kruk's head, all the way to the backstop. Kruk, a left-handed hitter, pantomimed a fluttering heart and comically bailed farther and farther out of the batter's box on each succeeding pitch. He finally struck out to end what he called "the worst at-bat of my life," and bowed in Randy's direction. After the inning, when Kruk walked past, Randy winked at him. Randy pitched two perfect innings in the game, and then looked skyward, a salute to his father.

Randy throws so hard that one of his biggest fears is a pitch getting away from him and hurting a player. He got a scare in July of 1993 when he hit Mike Greenwell of the Boston Red Sox on his helmet with a fastball. "I was so worried about what had happened and what Greenwell was going through I got an upset stomach from it," Randy said. Fortunately, Greenwell was not seriously hurt.

Randy had two other scary beanings in his career, hitting Jim Leyritz of the Yankees in 1995, and J.T. Snow of the Giants in spring training of 1997. Snow was the most seriously injured, fracturing his lower left eye orbit. Leyritz threatened retaliation, to which Randy responded with one of the most famous quotes of his career: "You can't intimidate the intimidator. I'm the intimidator. Jim Leyritz is the intimidatee."

In September of 1993, Randy got the ultimate compliment from his mentor, Nolan Ryan. "I thought Roger Clemens was the pitcher of the '80s," Ryan said. "Randy's the pitcher of the '90s. He is going to be the dominant pitcher. I don't see anybody else with his talent now."

The baseball strike of 1994 kept Randy from matching his numbers from the previous season, but he led the league in strikeouts again with 204 and went 13-6 with a league-leading four shutouts.

At times, it was a frustrating year for Randy, who spoke out when the Mariners fell 18 games under .500. He suggested the team might be better off to trade him. "I'm one of the best pitchers in baseball playing for one of the worst teams in baseball," he said. "From that standpoint, it gets frustrating when there's no hope for postseason play."

The Mariners didn't trade Randy, despite much more speculation throughout spring training of 1995, and his postseason frustrations soon ended. At peace with himself and now master of his craft,

In 1995, Randy won the American League Cy Young Award, while Mariners manager Lou Piniella, left, was named Manager of the Year and Edgar Martinez also of the Mariners was chosen as Designated Hitter of the Year. (AP/Wide World Photos)

Randy had a superb season, winning 18 games and losing just two as the Mariners roared from behind to the Western Division title. His winning percentage (.900) was an American League record, and his rate of 12.35 strikeouts per nine innings was a major-league mark.

Overall, Randy struck out 294 and walked just 65, causing former teammate Brian Holman to say, "Randy Johnson with control is almost unfair to a hitter."

After pitching Seattle to the title with his masterful playoff outing against the Angels, Randy wasn't through with his heroics. The Mariners lost the first two games of their best-of-five series with the Yankees, but Randy extended Seattle's season by pitching seven strong innings for a 7-4 win at the Kingdome. "I had the weight of all Washington on me, I felt," he said.

In the Mariners' 1995 Division Series against the Yankees, Randy pitched three innings of relief for a victory just 48 hours after winning Game 4. (AP/Wide World Photos)

If the Mariners were going to stay alive, it looked as if they would have to do it without Randy, who had thrown 116 pitches against the Yankees. But after they won Game 4, Randy told Piniella he was available to pitch in relief the next night if the Mariners needed him. Need him they did. Just 48 hours after his start, Randy worked three valiant innings of relief to earn the victory as Seattle clinched the series with a thrilling 6-5 win in 11 innings.

Randy struck out six, including all three outs in the 10th, but he actually was in line to lose the game when he gave up an RBI single in the 11th inning to Randy Velarde—the only hit he allowed —that put New York ahead, 5-4.

"I felt like I'd blown the game, blown the whole year," Randy said.

In the bottom of the 11th inning, Seattle's designated hitter Edgar Martinez ended one of the most

Greg Maddux, left, of the Atlanta Braves, won the National League Cy Young Award in 1995. Here, Greg and Randy pose for photographers. (AP/Wide World Photos)

exciting playoff games ever with a two-run double that scored Joey Cora from third and Ken Griffey Jr. from first.

"This team has won the four most important games in team history in the span of seven days," Piniella said, "and the Big Unit has won three of those. He's a horse. He's the best there is, and if I could reach him I'd probably kiss him. I was only going to use him for one inning, two tops. After he got through two innings, he wanted to go back out there."

Randy's extraordinary playoff run finally ended in the American League Championship Series, when the Cleveland Indians beat him 4-0 to clinch the pennant in the sixth game. But the Mariners' season was so successful that the state legislature voted them the funding for a new stadium, ensuring that the team wouldn't move. In November, the outcome of another vote was announced. With 26 of

28 first-place votes, Randy was the Cy Young Award winner. He had reached the top of his profession —but the biggest crisis of his career awaited him.

Turmoil and Triumph

Few thought much of it when Randy was sidelined early in spring training in 1996 because of a sore back. After all, Randy's back was sore every spring. It was one of the hazards of being a 6-10 pitcher and putting all that strain on his back. The Mariners assured people that he would be fine with a little rest.

But he wasn't fine. Oh, Randy started the season on schedule and got off to a brilliant start, winning his first five decisions. On Opening Night, he struck out 14 and allowed just three hits. But on April 26, he had to leave his start against Milwaukee in the fourth inning when his back acted up. "When I landed on my front foot, it was like a knife being jabbed in my back," he said.

Randy didn't know it yet, but that game was the beginning of an horrendous stretch that eventually wiped out the season. He made his next start against Texas but this time lasted only two innings.

The Mariners held him out for a start, but after pitching five innings to beat Kansas City on May 12, he was placed on the disabled list the following day. The diagnosis was a bulging disk that not only affected his back but caused shooting pain down his right leg. It would be nearly three months before he pitched again.

"I'd love to try to pitch but I can't," he said. "If I walk 100 yards to leave the Kingdome, I'm limping."

After a long period of rest and rehabilitation, the Mariners hoped Randy would not need surgery. He returned on August 6, and gave everyone cause for optimism. Working two innings of relief against Cleveland, he allowed just one hit and struck out four. He threw 29 pitches, and 22 were strikes. The Big Unit was back! "No one knows how hard I've worked to be ready," he said. "This was just one small step today."

The small step failed to lead to a giant leap. Randy teased fans with a strong outing on August 13 (eight strikeouts in four innings) for the second save of his career, but his next two appearances were rocky. The back was hurting him again, although some in the media criticized Randy for not attempting to start games.

On August 24, he allowed a grand slam to Boston's Darren Bragg, the first homer he had allowed to a left-handed hitter since 1992. Three days later, Randy was back on the disabled list, and this time doctors determined that he had a herniated disc that needed surgery.

On September 12, in Inglewood, California, Dr. Robert Watkins performed a micro-endoscopic discecktomy that involved removing an extruded piece of the disk in Johnson's fifth lumbar vertebra which had been pinching a nerve.

"We didn't find anything that would leave me to believe Randy's going to have any future problems," Dr. Watkins said. "I certainly expect a full recovery to his back problem."

Randy, naturally, was filled with anxiety about his future. His surgeon, he said, "is a doctor, not a miracle worker." When Randy woke up from the operation, he was so stiff and sore he couldn't even get out of bed. He wasn't worried about pitching again; he was just hoping he would be able to play with his children.

Randy underwent a rigorous winter rehabilitation program, and when spring training started, he reported on time with the other Mariner pitchers. Randy had played catch over the winter, but he hadn't yet thrown off a mound. Occasionally, he still had pain down his legs. He said his goal was to pitch Opening Day for the Mariners, but Randy had to admit, "I can't say now if I will be able to."

He told reporters, "It's been an emotional roller coaster, and I don't want to take that ride again. Some people in the media were skeptical of what I was going through, but no one knew what was really happening, that I tried to compete through the pain last year, that I'd come in between innings and lie with my legs raised to relieve the pain."

Randy told reporters how the uncertainty of his future even affected his relationship with Lisa. "My marriage was on the rocks for awhile," he said. "I was feeling a lot of anguish, and I was unfortunately taking it out on my wife, unintentionally....I must have been terrible to live with. But Lisa was as supportive as she could be through it all, and still is."

As it turned out, Randy wasn't quite ready for Opening Day because he had to proceed so slowly in spring training. Still, his comeback from surgery was a phenomenal success.

From nearly the moment he made his first start against Boston on April 5, it was clear that Randy was headed back to being the most dominating pitcher in the league. For proof, there was a one-hit shutout of Detroit, in which he struck out 15. Then came a 19-strikeout effort against Oakland, establishing an American League record for left-handers—and another 19-strikeout game against the White Sox, making him the first to record that many strikeouts in a game twice in a season. He was the winning pitcher when the Mariners beat the Angels to clinch another AL West title. In his final appearance of the season, Randy pitched two innings of relief against Oakland to wrap up the first 20-win season in Mariner history and rack up his 2,000th career strikeout. He did it despite missing four starts late in the season with a finger injury.

All in all, Randy went 20-4, giving him an astonishing 75-20 record since his career turnaround in 1993— a .789 winning percentage. His ERA of 2.28 was the lowest of his career, and he wound up with 291 strikeouts. Randy finished second in the Cy Young voting to Roger Clemens, who won the pitching "Triple Crown" by leading in wins, strikeouts and ERA.

For the second time, Randy was named the All-Star game starter, and he had another memorable confrontation with a left-handed hitter. This time it was Colorado's Larry Walker, a former teammate in the Expos' farm system, who had drawn criticism for asking to be benched when the Rockies faced Johnson earlier in the season in an interleague game. Once again, Randy threw a pitch that sailed high over the batter's head. Walker observed the next pitch from the right-handed batter's box. Randy finished with two shutout innings against the NL All-Stars.

The playoffs were not so triumphant. The Mariners were eliminated in the first round by Baltimore, and Randy lost both his starts to Orioles ace Mike Mussina. In the second one, Randy pitched a complete game and struck out 13, but Mussina was even better with a two-hitter.

Still, it was a highly successful season for Randy, who just a year earlier didn't know if he would ever pitch again.

"I feel with the back surgery and all the hard work I put in, essentially I'm a better pitcher now than I have ever been," he said.

There were other problems ahead, however. Randy's future with the Mariners was heading toward one final crisis.

Moving On

On November 12, 1997, the Mariners made a stunning announcement. It should have been a day for the organization to bask in the glory of Ken Griffey Jr.'s unanimous selection as American League MVP. Instead, the Mariners told fans that contract talks with Randy Johnson had broken down.

Randy was heading into the final year of his contract and hoped to get an extension that would allow him to remain in Seattle. Instead, Mariners president Chuck Armstrong said, "We have concluded that we are unable to offer Randy an extension of his contract beyond 1998. Therefore, our general manager, Woody Woodward, is free to entertain trade offers for him."

That news ensured that the 1998 season would be a tumultuous one for both Randy and the Mariners. Randy was already unhappy that the Mariners had waited until September before exercising his contract option for the 1998 season. He felt they had let him dangle too long. Now he was really left dangling. All winter long, trade rumors flew—Randy was going to Cleveland; he was going to the Yankees; he was going to the Dodgers; he was going to Toronto.

"I feel a little betrayed," Randy told the *Seattle Times.* "I feel like I've given my best years to date to the Mariners. I helped them save baseball in Seattle."

When spring training opened, Randy was still a Mariner. It was an uncomfortable situation, but he promised he wouldn't let the uncertainty disrupt his season. He issued a statement that said he would "focus all my energies on winning a world championship for Seattle fans." He said he was "upbeat and ready to go."

Randy's unclear status clearly affected him. When the season began—with trade rumors still flying—he was wildly inconsistent. At one point, when it looked like a deal with the Dodgers was near, he pitched back-to-back strong games against Tampa Bay, striking out 25 in 17 innings. That deal fell through at the last moment when an unnamed Mariner owner vetoed a trade that would have sent Randy to Los Angeles for pitcher Ismael Valdes, infielder Wilton Guerrero and a minor-league pitcher. Armstrong issued a statement that Randy wouldn't

On July 31, 1998, Randy was sent to the Houston Astros just hours before the trade deadline. (AP/Wide World Photos)

be traded. Randy, weary of constant speculation about his future, stopped talking to the media.

Meanwhile, Randy's inconsistency on the mound continued, and his frustration mounted. One day in July, Randy scuffled in the clubhouse with teammate David Segui. A few days later, he pitched a one-hit shutout against the Angels. When the July 31 trade deadline arrived, Randy had a 9-10 record and a 4.33 ERA. For the Mariners, it was now or never—trade Randy or keep him for the remainder of the season, at which point he would become a free agent.

The Mariners were playing that night at the Kingdome against the Yankees, one of the teams rumored to be pursuing Randy. At 9 p.m., the trade deadline passed without any word of a deal. Randy, who wasn't pitching that night, sat in the dugout and figured that the Mariners had been unable to trade him. A few minutes later, manager Piniella

Randy made his Astrodome debut in front of a sellout crowd and earned a shutout victory over the Philadelphia Phillies. (AP/Wide World Photos)

called him over and told him that he was heading to the Houston Astros. His Mariner career was over.

It turned out that Woodward had struck a deal with Houston G.M. Gerry Hunsicker at the last possible minute. In exchange for Randy, Seattle received three minor-leaguers—pitchers Freddy Garcia and John Halama, and second baseman Carlos Guillen. Just as they had been nine years earlier, when Langston was traded, Mariners fans were outraged.

"I would have loved to have been a Mariner forever and finished my career there," Randy told reporters when he arrived in Houston. "I feel bad for a lot of people. The Seattle fans. My teammates in Seattle. My family and myself."

Randy received a hero's welcome from the Astros, who were leading the National League's Central Division. "This ranks among the top five

Randy went 10-1 with a 1.28 ERA for the Astros. (AP/Wide World Photos)

or six events in Houston sports history," Hunsicker said.

Freed from the distractions in Seattle, Randy made an instant transformation to the overpowering Big Unit of old. He won his Astros debut by beating the Pittsburgh Pirates, striking out 10. In his first Astrodome start, a sellout crowd of 52,071 watched him pitch a five-hit shutout against the Phillies. It was the first of an incredible four straight shutouts he pitched at the Astrodome.

Overall with the Astros, Randy went 10-1 with an ERA of 1.28. After the trade, Houston went 22-7 in August, the best record for a single month in franchise history. They won the division title by 13 games. "He's exceeded all our expectations," Hunsicker said.

Despite his horrible start, Randy wound up with an overall 19-11 record in 1998. He struck out a career-high 329 batters, the most since Ryan

Randy, who became a free agent after the 1998 season, was eventually signed by the Arizona Diamondbacks for four years and $53 million. (AP/Wide World Photos)

fanned 341 in 1977. The Astros were counting on Randy leading them to their first World Series appearance, but the playoffs had a familiar ending for Randy. He pitched well, but his opponents pitched better.

The Astros were eliminated in four games by San Diego in the opening round, with Randy absorbing two of their three losses to extend his postseason losing streak to five games. He gave up a total of just three earned runs in 14 innings, but the Astros scored just two runs in the two games.

Now Randy faced a major decision: Where would he play in 1999? The drama played out much of the winter as several teams hotly pursued the free agent. The Astros made a bid to keep him. The Texas Rangers, Anaheim Angels, Los Angeles Dodgers, Baltimore Orioles and Arizona Diamondbacks all wanted to sign Randy.

*Randy tries on his new jersey at the press conference
announcing his signing with the Diamondbacks.
(AP/Wide World Photos)*

In the end, he picked the Diamondbacks, signing a four-year, $53-million contract on November 30. The one-year-old expansion team is located in Phoenix, where Randy and his family moved several years ago. Randy also was convinced that the Diamondbacks were on the verge of becoming a team that would contend for the National League pennant.

"I believe 110 percent I've made the right decision," he said. "A lot of people don't realize that what makes me tick out on the field is when I look up in the stands and I see my family up there. That really motivates me and makes me dig down a little deeper. I feel I can win here. I feel the team can win here, and I feel it's in the best interest of my family, too."

A new era for the Big Unit had begun.

Randy pauses a moment before pitching against the Padres in the 1998 National League Division Series. (AP/Wide World Photos)

Randy Johnson Quick Facts

Full Name:	Randall David Johnson
Team:	Arizona Diamondbacks
Hometown:	Walnut Creek, California
Position:	Pitcher
Jersey Number:	51
Bats:	Right
Throws:	Left
Height:	6-10
Weight:	225 pounds
Birthdate:	September 10, 1963

1998 Highlight: Helped lead the Houston Astros to the National League playoffs.

Stats Spotlight: With the Astros, he posted a 10-1 record and a 1.28 ERA, and struck out 116 batters in 84.1 innings.

Randy works out during spring training for the Diamondbacks. (AP/Wide World Photos)

Randy Johnson's Professional Career

Year	Club	W-L	ERA	G	GS	CG	SHO	SV	IP	H	R	ER	BB	SO
1988	Montreal	3-0	2.42	4	4	1	0	0	26	23	8	7	7	25
1989	Montreal	0-4	6.67	7	6	0	0	0	29.2	29	25	22	26	26
	Seattle	7-9	4.40	22	22	2	0	0	131	118	75	64	70	104
1990	Seattle	14-11	3.65	33	33	5	2	0	219.2	174	103	89	120*	194
1991	Seattle	13-10	3.98	33	33	2	1	0	201.1	151	96	89	152*	228
1992	Seattle	12-14	3.77	31	31	6	2	0	210.1	154	104	88	144*	241*
1993	Seattle	19-8	3.24	35	34	10	3	1	255.1	185	97	92	99	308*
1994	Seattle	13-6	3.19	23	23	9*	4*	0	172	132	65	61	72	204*
1995	Seattle	18-2	2.48*	30	30	6	3	0	214.1	159	65	59	65	294*
1996	Seattle	5-0	3.67	14	8	0	0	1	61.1	48	27	25	25	85
1997	Seattle	20-4	2.28	30	29	5	2	0	213	147	60	54	77	291
1998	Seattle	9-10	4.33	23	23	6	2	0	160	146	90	77	60	213
	Houston	10-1	1.28	11	11	4	4	0	84.1	57	12	12	26	116
M.L. Totals		143-79	3.36	296	287	56	23	2	1978.1	1523	827	739	943	2329

* Indicates League Leader

Active Career Strikeout Leaders

Roger Clemens	3153
Mark Langston	2421
Randy Johnson	**2329**
David Cone	2243
Dwight Gooden	2150
Greg Maddux	2024
Chuck Finley	1951

Active Career Strikeouts after Nine Innings Pitched

Randy Johnson	**10.60**
Hideo Nomo	9.98
Pedro Martinez	9.59
Randy Myers	8.99
Roger Clemens	8.67
Eric Plunk	8.52
Paul Assenmacher	8.51
Curt Schilling	8.45
David Cone	8.42
Dan Plesac	8.22

Active Career Winning Percentage

Mike Mussina	.667
Andy Pettitte	.657
Roger Clemens	.653
Pedro Martinez	.646
Randy Johnson	**.644**
David Cone	.644
Dwight Gooden	.642
Greg Maddux	.633
Tom Glavine	.622
Ramon Martinez	.615

Career Opponents Batting Average Leaders

Randy Johnson	**.212**
Pedro Martinez	.214
Mike Jackson	.216
Hideo Nomo	.218
Jesse Orosco	.219
David Cone	.224
Roger Clemens	.225
Jeff Brantley	.232
John Smoltz	.232
Randy Myers	.233

1990s American League Cy Young Award Winners

1998	Roger Clemens, Toronto
1997	Roger Clemens, Toronto
1996	Pat Hentgen, Toronto
1995	**Randy Johnson, Seattle**
1994	David Cone, New York
1993	Jack McDowell, Chicago
1992	Dennis Eckersley, Oakland
1991	Roger Clemens, Boston
1990	Bob Welch, Oakland

1995 American League Cy Young Award Voting

Player	Points
Randy Johson, Seattle	**136.0**
Jose Mesa, Cleveland	54.0
Tim Wakefield, Boston	29.0
David Cone, New ork	18.0
Mike Mussina, Baltimore	14.0
Charles Nagy, Cleveland	1.0

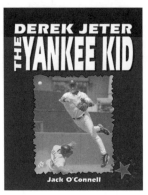

Derek Jeter:
The Yankee Kid
Author: Jack O'Connell
ISBN: 1-58261-043-6

In 1996 Derek burst onto the scene as one of the most promising young shortstops to hit the big leagues in a long time. His hitting prowess and ability to turn the double play have definitely fulfilled the early predictions of greatness.

A native of Kalamazoo, MI, Jeter has remained well grounded. He patiently signs autographs and takes time to talk to the young fans who will be eager to read more about him in this book.

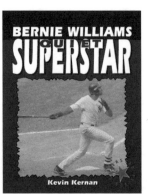

Bernie Williams:
Quiet Superstar
Author: Kevin Kernan
ISBN: 1-58261-044-4

Bernie Williams, a guitar-strumming native of Puerto Rico, is not only popular with his teammates, but is considered by top team officials to be the heir to DiMaggio and Mantle fame.

He draws frequent comparisons to Roberto Clemente, perhaps the greatest player ever from Puerto Rico. Like Clemente, Williams is humble, unassuming, and carries himself with quiet dignity. Also like Clemente, he plays with rare determination and a special elegance. He's married, and serves as a role model not only for his three children, but for his young fans here and in Puerto Rico.

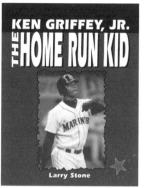

Ken Griffey, Jr.:
The Home Run Kid
Author: Larry Stone
ISBN: 1-58261-041-x

Capable of hitting majestic home runs, making breathtaking catches, and speeding around the bases to beat the tag by a split second, Ken Griffey, Jr. is baseball's Michael Jordan. Amazingly, Ken reached the Major Leagues at age 19, made his first All-Star team at 20, and produced his first 100 RBI season at 21.

The son of Ken Griffey, Sr., Ken is part of the only father-son combination to play in the same outfield together in the same game, and, like Barry Bonds, he's a famous son who turned out to be a better player than his father.

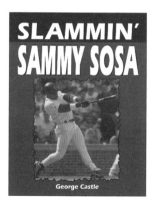

Sammy Sosa:
Slammin' Sammy
Author: George Castle
ISBN: 1-58261-029-0

1998 was a break-out year for Sammy as he amassed 66 home runs, led the Chicago Cubs into the playoffs and finished the year with baseball's ultimate individual honor, MVP.

When the national spotlight was shone on Sammy during his home run chase with Mark McGwire, America got to see what a special person he is. His infectious good humor and kind heart have made him a role model across the country.

Nomar Garciaparra: High 5!

Author: Mike Shalin
ISBN: 1-58261-053-3

An All-American at Georgia Tech, a star on the 1992 U.S. Olympic Team, the twelfth overall pick in the 1994 draft, and the 1997 American League Rookie of the Year, Garciaparra has exemplified excellence on every level.

At shortstop, he'll glide deep into the hole, stab a sharply hit grounder, then throw out an opponent on the run. At the plate, he'll uncoil his body and deliver a clutch double or game-winning homer. Nomar is one of the game's most complete players.

Juan Gonzalez: Juan Gone!

Author: Evan Grant
ISBN: 1-58261-048-7

One of the most prodigious and feared sluggers in the major leagues, Gonzalez was a two-time home run king by the time he was 24 years old.

After having something of a personal crisis in 1996, the Puerto Rican redirected his priorities and now says baseball is the third most important thing in his life after God and family.

Mo Vaughn:
Angel on a Mission
Author: Mike Shalin
ISBN: 1-58261-046-0

Growing up in Connecticut, this Angels slugger learned the difference between right and wrong and the value of honesty and integrity from his parents early on, lessons that have stayed with him his whole life.

This former American League MVP was so active in Boston charities and youth programs that he quickly became one of the most popular players ever to don the Red Sox uniform.

Mo will be a welcome addition to the Angels line-up and the Anaheim community.

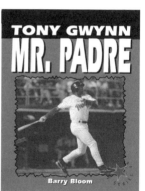

Tony Gwynn:
Mr. Padre
Author: Barry Bloom
ISBN: 1-58261-049-5

Tony is regarded as one of the greatest hitters of all-time. He is one of only three hitters in baseball history to win eight batting titles (the others: Ty Cobb and Honus Wagner).

In 1995 he won the Branch Rickey Award for Community Service by a major leaguer. He is unfailingly humble and always accessible, and he holds the game in deep respect. A throwback to an earlier era, Gwynn makes hitting look effortless, but no one works harder at his craft.

Sandy and Roberto Alomar:
Baseball Brothers

Author: Barry Bloom
ISBN: 1-58261-054-1

Sandy and Roberto Alomar are not just famous baseball brothers they are also famous baseball sons. Sandy Alomar, Sr. played in the major leagues fourteen seasons and later went into management. His two baseball sons have made names for themselves and have appeared in multiple All-Star games.

With Roberto joining Sandy in Cleveland, the Indians look to be a front-running contender in the American League Central.

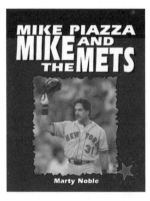

Mike Piazza:
Mike and the Mets

Author: Marty Noble
ISBN: 1-58261-051-7

A total of 1,389 players were selected ahead of Mike Piazza in the 1988 draft, who wasn't picked until the 62nd round, and then only because Tommy Lasorda urged the Dodgers to take him as a favor to his friend Vince Piazza, Mike's father.

Named in the same breath with great catchers of another era like Bench, Dickey and Berra, Mike has proved the validity of his father's constant reminder "If you work hard, dreams do come true."

Curt Schilling: Phillie Phire!

Author: Paul Hagen
ISBN: 1-58261-055-x

Born in Anchorage, Alaska, Schilling has found a warm reception from the Philadelphia Phillies faithful. He has amassed 300+ strikeouts in the past two seasons and even holds the National League record for most strikeouts by a right handed pitcher at 319.

This book tells of the difficulties Curt faced being traded several times as a young player, and how he has been able to deal with off-the-field problems.

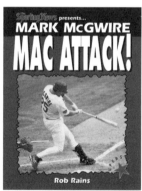

Mark McGwire: Mac Attack!

Author: Rob Rains
ISBN: 1-58261-004-5

Mac Attack! describes how McGwire overcame poor eyesight and various injuries to become one of the most revered hitters in baseball today. He quickly has become a legendary figure in St. Louis, the home to baseball legends such as Stan Musial, Lou Brock, Bob Gibson, Red Schoendienst and Ozzie Smith. McGwire thought about being a police officer growing up, but he hit a home run in his first Little League at-bat and the rest is history.

Roger Clemens: Rocket Man!

Author: Kevin Kernan
ISBN: 1-58261-128-9

Alex Rodriguez: A-plus Shortstop

ISBN: 1-58261-104-1

SUPERSTAR SERIES

Collect Them All!

Baseball
SuperStar Series Titles

____ Sandy and Roberto Alomar:
Baseball Brothers

____ Kevin Brown: Kevin with a "K"

____ Roger Clemens: Rocket Man!

____ Juan Gonzalez: Juan Gone!

____ Mark Grace: Winning With Grace

____ Ken Griffey, Jr.: The Home Run Kid

____ Tony Gwynn: Mr. Padre

____ Derek Jeter: The Yankee Kid

____ Randy Johnson: Arizona Heat!

____ Pedro Martinez: Throwing Strikes

____ Mike Piazza: Mike and the Mets

____ Alex Rodriguez: A-plus Shortstop

____ Curt Schilling: Philly Phire!

____ Sammy Sosa: Slammin' Sammy

____ Mo Vaughn: Angel on a Mission

____ Omar Vizquel:
The Man with a Golden Glove

____ Larry Walker: Colorado Hit Man!

____ Bernie Williams: Quiet Superstar

____ Mark McGwire: Mac Attack!

Available by calling 877-424-BOOK